W9-CDY-680

Walt Disney's

The JungleBook

Mowgli had lived with the wolves since he was a baby. He howled, scratched, and wrestled with the wolf pups. The jungle was his home. But as Mowgli grew, his wolf parents were worried for his safety.

The tiger, Shere Khan, had sworn to kill the boy. Shere Khan was afraid of man's guns and fire, and he feared Mowgli would grow up to be a hunter. For Mowgli's protection, the wolves thought it best for him to go live in the Man-village with his own kind.

One day, a friend came to the wolves' den. It was Bagheera, the panther. He took Mowgli for a long walk. When it grew dark, Mowgli yawned. "I'm getting a little sleepy," he said. "Shouldn't we start back home?"

"Mowgli, this time we're not going back," said Bagheera. "I'm taking you to the Man-village. Shere Khan has returned to this part of the jungle.

"We'll spend the night here," the panther added, as he and Mowgli climbed up to a high tree branch.

As Bagheera drifted off to sleep, a snake named Kaa slithered through the leaves.

"Go away!" Mowgli told the python, but Kaa was hungry. He looked deeply into Mowgli's eyes, hypnotizing him. Then he started to wrap his body around the boy!

Just then, Bagheera opened his eyes. "Kaa!" cried Bagheera, swiping at the snake with his paw. Startled, Mowgli snapped out of the trance. Then the boy shoved the snake out of the tree. Mowgli laughed as Kaa slithered away, his tail tied into a knot.

Later that night, Mowgli ran away from Bagheera. I can take care of myself, he thought. Luckily, Mowgli was not alone in the dangerous jungle for long. He met a friendly bear named Baloo.

"Hey, kid, you need help," said the bear, "and old Baloo's gonna learn you to fight like a bear."

And so he did. Soon Mowgli and Baloo were laughing and playing like old friends. They ate bananas, scratched their backs on trees, and floated down the river, humming happy tunes.

One day, some orangutans swung down from the trees, and grabbed Mowgli. "Give me back my Man-cub!" cried Baloo.

But the orangutans escaped into the jungle with Mowgli. They brought the Man-cub to their leader, King Louie. The king sat on his throne inside some ancient ruins. He promised to help Mowgli stay in the jungle if the boy would teach him how to make fire.

Soon the orangutans started dancing, and a party began. Then a mysterious new orangutan joined the group. But as King Louie danced with the newcomer, her costume fell to the ground. It was really Baloo! He grabbed Mowgli and raced out of the temple.

The next morning, Baloo sadly explained to Mowgli that he could not keep the boy safe from Shere Khan. Mowgli belonged in the Man-village.

Feeling betrayed, Mowgli ran away again. He ran until he couldn't hear Baloo calling him anymore. Then Mowgli sat down and started to cry.

Suddenly, Shere Khan bounded out of the jungle! He was after Mowgli! But Baloo had caught up just in time. He grabbed the tiger by his tail. Around and around they ran. Finally, Shere Khan broke loose. He was furious! With his sharp claws bared, the tiger attacked Baloo.

Thunder roared and lightning flashed. All of a sudden, a bolt of lightning struck a dead tree. With a loud hiss, the tree burst into flames.

Mowgli saw his chance! He grabbed a burning branch and tied it to Shere Khan's tail. And with one last terrified roar, the mighty tiger ran away into the jungle.

Later, as Mowgli hugged Baloo, they heard a strange sound. It was singing—a girl singing.

Mowgli climbed out onto a tree branch to get a closer look. He had never seen another human before. He was entranced. When the girl smiled at him, Mowgli followed her to the Man-village.

As Mowgli looked back to say good-bye, he knew Baloo and Bagheera were right: this was the way it should be. But the jungle—and his jungle friends— would always remain in his heart.